Andi's Indian Summer

Circle C Beginnings Series

Circle C Beginnings

Andi's Indian Summer

Susan K. Marlow
Illustrated by Leslie Gammelgaard

Kregel
Publications

Andi's Indian Summer
©2010 by Susan K. Marlow

Illustrations ©2010 by Leslie Gammelgaard

Published by Kregel Publications, a division of Kregel, Inc.,
P.O. Box 2607, Grand Rapids, MI 49501.

The persons and events portrayed in this work are the creations of the author, and any resemblance to persons living or dead is purely coincidental.

Library of Congress Cataloging-in-Publication Data
Marlow, Susan K.
    Andi's Indian summer / Susan K. Marlow ; illustrated by
Leslie Gammelgaard.
        p. cm. — (Circle C beginnings series ; [1])
1. Yokuts Indians—Juvenile fiction. [1. Yokuts Indians—
Fiction. 2. Indians of North America—California—
Fiction. 3. Ranch life—California—Fiction. 4. California—
History—1846-1850—Fiction.] I. Gammelgaard, Leslie,
ill. II. Title.
PZ7.M34528An   2010   [Fic]—dc22   2010033905

ISBN 978-0-8254-4182-0

Printed in the United States of America
12 13 14 15 / 6 5 4

Contents

New Words

captive	a person who is kept in a place where he or she does not want to be
cookhouse	a building used for cooking, where the cowboys eat their meals
cowboys	the men who work on a ranch
hayloft	the place upstairs in the barn where hay is kept
jim-dandy	very good; great
mush	hot cereal
novel	a long story; a book
ohóm	the Yokut word for "no"
pasture	a grassy field for horses and cows
Yokut	a peaceful Indian tribe in California

Chapter 1

Too Busy

"Hey, Andi!" Riley yelled. "Come see what I have."

Andi did not want to see what her friend Riley had. Not today. She was too busy. She was leading her very own baby horse, Taffy, around the pasture.

Taffy's mama, Snowflake, was helping. Sometimes Taffy didn't want to follow Andi. When that happened, Snowflake gave her baby a push with her big, white nose.

Obey Andi! Snowflake seemed to be saying.

Riley climbed over the rail fence and jumped down. "Did you hear me, Andi? I've got something to show you."

Riley *always* had something to show Andi. Sometimes he showed her a new riding trick. Sometimes he pulled a frog or a snake out of his pocket.

Just last week, Riley showed her a new litter of kittens in the barn.

Most of the time, Andi liked to see what Riley had in his pockets. She liked to watch him do tricks on Midnight, his big, black horse.

But not today.

"I'm busy," Andi said. She pulled on Taffy's lead rope and kept walking. "I'm training Taffy. All by myself. Chad said I could."

Andi felt a lot bigger than six years old today. For once, her big brother Chad was not helping with Taffy. He was too busy. He said Andi could do it if she was careful.

Andi wanted to be careful with Taffy. She wanted to show Chad she could do everything just right. No mistakes. Then Chad would let her train Taffy by herself on other days.

Maybe.

Andi was much too busy to look at anything Riley had. Even if he had a fat, green, extra-jumpy frog to show her.

Riley ran across the pasture and grabbed her arm. "You have to see what one of the cowboys gave me."

Andi stopped. She couldn't walk very far with a big, eight-year-old boy holding her arm.

Taffy stopped walking too.

Andi smiled and patted Taffy. "Good girl."

"Don't you want to see what I have?" Riley asked.

Andi frowned. It looked like Riley was not going to leave her alone. "What is it?"

Riley let go of Andi's arm. He reached into his back pocket. Then he pulled out a wad of rolled-up papers. It looked like a book.

Andi wrinkled her eyebrows. *A book?*

Books did not make Andi feel very excited—especially since she couldn't read.

Andi squinted at the yellow-brown book in Riley's hand. It looked old and worn out. It looked like hundreds and hundreds of people had read it before Riley got it.

She let out a big breath. "What makes you think I want to look at a book?"

Riley bent close to Andi's ear, like he was telling her an important secret.

"This isn't just *any* book," he whispered. "It's a . . . *dime novel.*"

Andi didn't say anything. She didn't know what Riley was talking about. It looked like a plain old book to her.

What was so secret about that?

She shrugged. "So what?"

"Don't you know what a dime novel is?"

Riley asked. Then he laughed. "*Everybody* knows about dime novels."

Andi scowled. She didn't know what a dime novel was. And she didn't care, either.

Andi was not going to stand around and let Riley laugh at her. She was not going to let him show off that he knew something she didn't know.

Not for even one minute.

"Come on, Taffy," she said, pulling on the lead rope. "Let's get away from Mr. Too-Big-for-His-Britches. He thinks he knows everything."

"Wait!" Riley said. He started talking fast. "It's a book with a paper cover that costs one dime. Just ten cents. The inside pages are a little worn out, but take a look at this cover."

Riley stuck the book in Andi's face.

That got her attention.

The cover of Riley's book was full of bright colors and scary-looking Indians. The Indians had war paint on their faces. They were sneaking up on somebody.

Andi's heart started beating fast.

She had never, ever seen a book like this before!

Chapter 2

Dime Novel

Andi dropped Taffy's lead rope and gasped. She suddenly wished she knew how to read.

"What does it say?" she asked.

Riley pointed to some black letters on the cover. "**The Indian Captive**," he read. "Isn't that a jim-dandy name for a book?"

"The Indian captive," Andi said softly.

Andi knew what an Indian captive was. It was when you had to live with the Indians. Even if you didn't want to. Only, she didn't know why the Indians would want to capture somebody and take them far away.

That sounded mean . . . and scary.

Andi pushed the book away and picked up Taffy's lead rope. "It's just an old book," she said. "And I can't read."

She didn't want to tell Riley that it looked like a scary book.

"Dime novel, Andi," Riley said. "It's a *dime novel*. It says so right on the cover. Dime novels are different than other books. Dime novels are full of adventure—not like the books at school."

Riley made a face to show Andi what he thought about school books.

Andi perked up. *Full of adventure!* That sounded exciting. Andi loved adventure.

Even if it might be a little bit scary.

Every night before bed, Andi's sister Melinda read out loud from a book with no pictures. Andi didn't know what was going on in that book. She always fell asleep when Melinda was reading.

"I wouldn't fall asleep if Melinda was reading this dime novel," she said.

"Nope," Riley agreed. "You sure wouldn't. You would stay awake for sure."

He rolled the book up and stuffed it back

in his pocket. "If you want, I can read it to you sometime. I read real good."

"Is that why you didn't have to go to school last year?" Andi wanted to know. "'Cause you can already read?"

A sudden idea popped into her head. Maybe if Riley taught her to read, she wouldn't have to go to school in the fall.

Before she could tell him her great idea, Riley laughed. "Even if you can read, you still have to go to school. But Uncle Sid lets me work on your ranch instead. He's the best uncle in the whole world!"

Then Riley stopped laughing. His eyes turned sad. "When my mother gets well, I'll go home," he said softly. "Then I'll have to go back to school."

Andi did not want Riley to leave the ranch. Not ever. He was a good friend. He let her ride Midnight. He made her laugh.

Andi felt a little sad inside. She knew Riley missed his mother. He had to live with his Uncle Sid, the ranch boss, until she was well again.

"When I say my prayers at night, I always

say one for your mother," Andi said. *Even though I don't want you to leave the ranch.*

But she didn't say that part out loud.

"Thanks," Riley said. He pulled out the book again. "Do you want me to read it right now? You'll like it. It's exciting."

Andi frowned. She did not want to stop training Taffy. She wanted to lead her little foal around the pasture all day long.

But then she looked up. The sun was high in the sky. It was almost lunchtime. She remembered what Chad told her at breakfast.

Go slow, Andi. Train Taffy a little bit at a time. Don't wear her out.

For once, Chad did not sound bossy. He sounded like he knew what he was talking about.

"Okay," Andi said. "We can go up in the hayloft. You can read me your dime novel while I play with the kittens."

Riley gave Andi a big smile. Then he dashed to the fence. "Hurry up!" he yelled.

Andi did not feel like hurrying up. She was not sure she wanted to hear a book about Indian captives.

Even if Riley said the book was exciting and full of adventure.

She took off Taffy's halter. "You can play with Coco until I get back," she said.

Taffy galloped over to her mother. But before she took a drink of her mother's warm milk, the baby horse touched noses with Andi's pony, Coco.

"Maybe you can make Coco gallop," Andi told Taffy. "Then he won't be so pokey."

She waved good-bye, climbed over the fence, and skipped all the way to the barn.

Riley was waiting for her.

Andi climbed the ladder to the hayloft. She picked up a kitten and plopped down in the dry, golden hay.

The hay smelled good—just like summertime.

The kitten purred.

Andi felt sleepy. Training Taffy was a lot of work.

But as soon as Riley started reading, Andi's eyes popped wide open.

Riley was right. His dime novel was full of adventure. It was exciting. Indians rushed around. They sneaked up on people in their cabins. They captured them.

Then Riley stopped reading. He looked at Andi.

Andi felt shivers go up and down her arms, but she said, "Keep reading, Riley!"

So he did.

Chapter 3

Daydreaming

Andi felt a sharp tug on her braid.

"Ow!" she hollered. She jumped up from the table as fast as she could. An Indian was trying to capture her! She had to get away!

But Andi jumped up too fast.

Her chair fell over with a *crash!* Soup splashed out of her bowl. Her glass of milk tipped over and spilled across the clean, white tablecloth.

Splash! The milk landed in her sister's lap.

"Andi!" Melinda screeched. She jumped up as fast as Andi did.

Andi blinked.

The Indians inside her head faded away. She wasn't in a cabin, being sneaked up on. She wasn't in the hayloft, listening to Riley read that scary dime novel.

She was eating lunch with her family. Safe!

Andi's pounding heart slowed down.

But not for long.

"Look what you did!" Melinda yelled.

Andi looked around the table. What a mess! Nobody was smiling. Everybody looked very surprised.

"I'm sorry," Andi said in a tiny voice. "It was . . . an accident."

"Andrea, what's the matter?" Mother asked. She began mopping up the drippy mess.

Melinda and Justin helped her.

Andi's cheeks felt hot. "I . . . I . . ."

She didn't know what to say. How do you tell your mother that an Indian was sneaking up on you?

Just then Andi saw her brother Mitch. He was sitting right next to her. *He* must have pulled her braid! What kind of mean trick was that?

Andi picked up her chair. Then she sat down and scowled at Mitch. "Why did you pull my hair?"

"I'm sorry, Andi," Mitch said. "I didn't know you would be so jumpy. I asked you three times to pass the salt. But you just kept staring at your soup."

Then Mitch grinned. "You were daydreaming. I figured a little tug on your braid might wake you up."

"You sure *did* wake her up, Mitch," Melinda said. "She spilled milk all over my dress." She crossed her arms and sat down hard.

Andi's cheeks got even hotter. She stared at her lap and didn't say a word.

"What were you daydreaming about, honey?" Justin asked.

Andi looked up.

Justin was smiling at her in a nice way. He looked interested in what she had to say. That's why she loved her oldest brother so much. He listened to her—just like Father used to do, before he died in a roundup accident.

But Andi didn't want to tell *anybody* about Riley's scary dime novel.

Not even Justin.

Just then Chad started laughing. "From the way she jumped, it looks to me like she's in some kind of trouble. Did Sid get after you today, Andi?"

"No!" Andi hollered.

She didn't care if she was shouting at the table. Bossy Chad always thought she was doing something that caused trouble.

"Don't tease her, Chad," Mother said. "There's no harm done. A little spilled milk is nothing to fuss over. And daydreaming never hurt anybody."

Andi was glad Mother wasn't upset about the mess.

But Andi wasn't so sure that daydreaming never hurt anybody.

She wished Riley had not read her that dime novel. Now she could not get all those word pictures about Indians out of her head. They were stuck—just like a sticky piece of taffy candy in her hair.

Would those word pictures *ever* go away?

Or would Indians keep sneaking around inside her head? Would they pop out and scare her in the middle of the night?

Scary old dime novel.

Chapter 4

Cook

After lunch, Andi wanted to go outside.

She wanted to get away from spilled soup and messy milk. She wanted to forget about mean brothers who pulled her braids and scared her.

Even if it wasn't on purpose.

Andi picked up her dishes and headed for the kitchen in a hurry. She couldn't wait to get outside!

"Be careful," Mother said. "Let's not have any more spills today—or any broken dishes."

Andi slowed down a little bit. She carried her dishes to the kitchen and set them down. She tried to be careful. She did not want to break any dishes.

Broken dishes might make Mother grumpy.

Andi didn't want to make Mother grumpy. Not today. Not when she had an important question to ask her.

Her words came out all in a rush. "Can I take Taffy riding with me? She's big enough. Chad said so. Please, Mother? I'll ride Coco. Taffy follows Coco everywhere. They're friends. The best friends ever. Taffy will stay by Coco. I know she will."

Andi stopped and took a breath.

"*May* I take Taffy," Mother corrected.

Andi nodded. "May I take her? Please?"

"Is Riley or Melinda going along on this ride?" Mother asked.

"Riley is. As soon as he finishes his chores for Cook. *May* I take Taffy? Riley will help me. Please?"

"If Chad told you it's all right then yes, you may," Mother said, smiling. "But make sure you look after Taffy. Don't let her get too tired."

Andi threw her arms around Mother. "I'll take care of her. I promise. Thank you!"

Then Andi dashed out the back door. She slammed the door shut and jumped off the porch in one giant leap.

"Riley!" she shouted.

There was no answer.

It was way past lunchtime. The cowboys were done eating. Riley must be finished with his chores. Where was he?

"Riley!" Andi called again. She ran to the cookhouse, stepped up on the porch, and reached for the doorknob.

Just as she turned the knob, the door flew open. Andi tumbled to the floor. *Ouch!*

She looked up. Riley and the ranch cook were standing there.

Cook was an old man. His brown face was full of wrinkles. He had dark, bushy eyebrows that almost hid his black eyes. Right now those black eyes were glaring at Andi.

Crashing into the cookhouse was maybe not a good idea.

She jumped to her feet and gave Cook a tiny smile. "Sorry, Cook."

Cook had another name. It was a Mexican name that Andi could never remember.

But everybody on the ranch just called him "Cook."

Most of the time Cook spoke Spanish, and Andi talked to Cook in Spanish.

But not today.

Cook put his wrinkled, brown hands on his hips and yelled, "You kids get out of here before I skin you alive! I got work to do."

"Skin you alive" were Cook's favorite English words. He said them a lot—mostly to Riley.

Riley raised his eyebrows at Cook. "I can go? I don't have to dry the dishes? Or bring you more firewood? Or scrub the tables?"

Cook waved his arms and said a few words in Spanish. Then he shoved Andi and Riley out the door.

Andi giggled. "Cook told us to go play." She hopped off the porch. "Cook is nicer than he looks, I think."

"To you, maybe," Riley said. "But Cook's bossy. And he always tells me that he's going to skin me alive."

"Cook doesn't mean it," Andi said. "That's just something he likes to say."

For once, Andi felt smarter than Riley.

"Maybe," Riley said. "But being skinned alive sounds scary."

He pulled the dime novel out of his pocket. "I think I'd rather be captured by Indians, like in this book. I'd live with the tribe and turn into an Indian boy. I'd ride an Indian pony and learn to hunt with a bow and—"

Andi covered her ears.

"What's wrong?" Riley asked.

"I don't want to talk about being captured by Indians." She felt a little shaky inside. "And I don't think I like that dime novel. It's . . . it's . . . disgusting."

Disgusting is what Melinda said whenever Andi showed her a frog or a spider or a lizard.

Riley laughed. "Really? You liked it good enough when I was reading it. In fact, you told me to keep reading."

"I changed my mind," Andi said. "Put it away."

"Too bad," Riley said, stuffing the book in his back pocket. "I think you would make a good Indian captive. You have dark braids just like an Indian girl. If you got captured, nobody would even know that you're not—"

"Don't say that!" Andi yelled.

Then she turned her back on Riley and stomped away.

Chapter 5

Afternoon Ride

Andi wanted to stay mad at Riley. He was mean to say she would make a good Indian captive.

But if she stayed mad he might not go riding with her. And she would rather go riding than stay mad.

So Andi helped Riley drag the reins and the bridles and the brushes from the barn to the pasture.

Coco gave a happy whinny when he saw Andi. He trotted over to the fence and pricked up his ears. He liked to be brushed. He liked to take Andi riding.

Andi did not like to ride Coco. He was a slowpoke. Andi wanted to go fast—as fast as the wind.

But she did not tell Coco this. Not today. It might hurt his feelings, and Coco was her friend. Besides, Taffy was coming, so Andi had to ride slow.

Even if she didn't want to.

Andi grabbed the brush, climbed over the fence, and brushed the dust off her pony's back. Then she combed out his long, brown mane.

"Taffy is coming with us today, Coco," she said. "You have to help me look after her. We can't let her get lost. Promise? Promise to help me?"

Coco tossed his head up and down.

"Good boy," Andi said, giving him a pat.

Riley laughed. "Coco didn't understand you. He tossed his head because you yanked on a tangle."

Andi pretended Riley didn't say that. Of course Coco understood what she told him! He might be an old, hand-me-down pony, but he was smart.

Maybe even smarter than Riley, she thought.

Riley opened the gate and led Midnight out of the pasture. Andi led Coco out.

Then Andi called, "Come on, Taffy! Come for a gallop with us."

Quick as a wink, Taffy chased after Coco. She didn't even look back at her mother, Snowflake. Taffy liked to be with Coco, her pasture pal.

Snowflake started trotting toward the gate. She whinnied.

But Riley shut the gate just in time. Now Snowflake could not get out.

Andi climbed on Coco's back and picked up the reins. "Let's go, Coco."

Coco started off at a slow walk, just like a turtle.

Andi didn't like to walk, so she gave Coco a little kick. Her pony broke into a bouncy trot. Andi was used to that, even if she didn't like it.

Just then Andi saw a blur of gold and white running beside her. It was Taffy. Her little horse was growing fast! She was almost as big as Coco.

And it looked like she could run fast.

Taffy kicked up her feet and ran faster. She galloped way past Coco. She galloped to where Riley and Midnight were riding far ahead.

"Come back, Taffy!" Andi called. Her heart thumped. Taffy could not run off whenever she wanted. She might get lost.

Then Andi got the surprise of her life.

Coco's bouncy trot turned smooth and fast. Coco was galloping! He was galloping after Taffy!

"Look, Riley!" Andi shouted. "Taffy got Coco to gallop!"

She laughed. Galloping Coco was so much fun!

But Andi's fast ride did not last long.

Coco gave a loud whinny, and Taffy stopped galloping.

Just like that.

The baby horse turned around and trotted back to Coco.

Coco slowed down to a bouncy trot, and Taffy stayed right next to him.

"Your gallop didn't last very long," Riley said when Andi caught up. "But at least you know Taffy obeys Coco. That's a good thing. Coco will keep Taffy out of trouble."

Andi wanted to gallop Coco, but she knew Riley was right. Taffy's first time outside the pasture had to go just right. If Taffy always stayed close to Coco, then Chad would let Andi take Taffy out again and again.

All summer long.

Andi and Riley trotted their horses for a long time. Pretty soon Andi couldn't see the ranch house or the barn or the cookhouse.

The flat land began to turn into a lot of little hills. The hills were golden, with oak trees growing all over them.

"Are we going to the meadow?" Andi asked. She knew where to find the meadow. She rode Coco there all the time.

"I have a better idea," Riley said. "Let's go to the creek."

Andi gave a little gasp. "The creek's too far away! It will take a long time to get there."

"No, it won't," Riley said. "It just seems far 'cause you're little. It's not too far for me."

"I'm *not* little," Andi said in a huff. "And if it's not too far for you, then it's not too far for *me*."

Riley grinned. "Okay, let's go."

Chapter 6

The Creek

"Riley's acting too big for his britches again," Andi told Coco in a grumpy voice.

It was bad enough when Andi's grown-up brothers called her *baby sister*. But when Riley said she was little, it really made her mad.

She gave Coco an extra-hard kick, and the pony took off. Andi bounced around on Coco's slippery brown back.

Taffy leaped and ran ahead to Midnight. Then she galloped back to Coco. It looked like the little foal was having a good time.

But not for long.

The sun grew hot. It beat down on Andi's head. She wished she had a drink of water. She wished she could dunk her head in water.

Taffy stopped running and jumping. She walked slower. Taffy needed a drink of water too.

"I'm hot," Andi grumbled. "The creek's a long way, but I don't remember it being *this* far away."

"That's because you never have to trot all the way by yourself," Riley said. "You always ride with somebody else on a fast horse."

Riley was right about that. Andi always rode to the creek with Mitch or Melinda. She had never ridden Coco to the creek.

Just then a scary thought popped into Andi's head. She didn't even know where this creek was.

She looked at Riley. "You know where the creek is, right?"

"Of course I do," Riley said. He pointed to a hill with a bunch of trees sticking out of it. "See over there? The creek is on the other side of that hill."

Andi looked around. All the hills looked alike to her. "Are you sure?"

"Sure I'm sure!" Riley said crossly. He sounded tired. And hot.

Andi followed Riley around the hill. She shaded her eyes and looked everywhere. There was no creek. She only saw more hills. *Lots* of hills.

"Where's the creek?" she asked.

For once, Riley didn't say anything. He stared at the hills. He stared at the trees. Then he looked up, as if the creek might be hiding in the bright blue sky.

Andi looked up too. "Why are you looking at the sky?"

"So I can see where the sun is," Riley explained. "It shows me which way to go."

"I don't care where the sun is," Andi grouched. "I want to know where the *creek* is. I'm thirsty. Taffy's thirsty. And . . ." She sniffed. No tears! Not in front of Riley.

"I know where I'm going!" Riley hollered.

It didn't look that way to Andi.

Riley turned Midnight in a different direction. He waved at Andi. "Come on."

Andi sighed. She had to do what Riley told her. He was bigger and older. She didn't want to be left behind, so she trotted after Midnight.

Taffy followed, but her head hung down. Her tail looked droopy.

Andi blinked back a few tears. If Taffy got tired, Chad would never let Andi take her out again.

"I want to go home," she said.

"Not until we find the creek," Riley told her.

Finally, after a long time, Riley gave a big whoop. "Look over there, Andi! Look at all those bushes and trees. That's the creek. I know it is."

Riley was right.

Nothing in the whole world looked better to Andi than that bubbling creek. She slid off Coco's back and ran to the water. She pulled off her boots and socks. She rolled up her overall legs. She rolled up her sleeves.

Then *splash!* Andi jumped in the creek. She took a long drink of water.

Riley waded into the creek and splashed Andi.

Andi splashed him back.

Midnight and Coco stepped into the creek. They drank the cool, fresh water.

Even Taffy got wet. She put her head down and drank for a long time. Then she nibbled at the grass that grew next to the creek.

Andi forgot about being hot and thirsty.
She forgot about Taffy being tired. She forgot
about wanting to go home. It was too much fun
splashing and playing in the creek.

"Close your eyes and hold out your hands,"
Riley said a long time later.

Andi looked up from trying to catch a water

bug. Riley was hiding something behind his back.

She shut her eyes.

Riley plopped something big and wet and slippery in her hands.

Andi's eyes flew open. She stared at the biggest frog she had ever seen. It took both hands to hold it.

Andi giggled. But she didn't say a word. She and Riley stood still and admired the frog in Andi's hands.

The creek made splashing noises, but there was no other sound. Even the tree leaves were quiet.

It was a perfect afternoon at a perfect creek, with a perfect frog.

Then . . . *crack!*

A branch snapped. Then another. The crackling noises came from the thick bushes a little way up the creek.

Something was moving in those bushes!

Chapter 7

Snapping and Crackling

"What's making that noise?" Andi whispered. Her heart went *thump-thump-thump.*

Riley looked at the bushes. Then he wrinkled his eyebrows. "It's probably just a rabbit. Or a beaver. Or maybe a . . . skunk." He pinched his nose and made a funny face.

Riley didn't look scared. He looked silly.

Andi laughed.

The horses were looking at the bushes too. Their ears twitched. They stood still and listened.

The snapping sounds grew louder.

"It sounds bigger than a skunk," Andi said. "You don't think it's . . . it's . . ."

She stopped talking.

"What?" Riley asked.

"I-Indians?" Andi whispered. Her heart *really* began to thump.

Then her hands got shaky, and she dropped the frog.

Plop! The frog hit the water and started swimming across the creek.

"Hey!" Riley yelled. He went splashing after the frog.

But the frog could swim fast. It found a hidey-hole and disappeared before Riley could catch it.

Riley splashed back to Andi and put his hands on his hips. He looked very cross.

"That frog was a beauty, and now it's gone," he said. "All because you're scared of a little noise."

"I'm *not* scared!" Andi shouted back.

Only, that wasn't exactly true.

Riley shook his head. "Indians in the bushes. That's just plain silly."

"It's your fault for reading me that *disgusting* dime novel," Andi said.

She climbed out of the creek in a huff. Then she plopped on the ground next to Taffy, who was lying down. She frowned at Riley to show him how mad she was.

But she couldn't stop thinking about Indians.

The bushes snapped and crackled some more.

Andi wrapped her fingers around Taffy's short, curly mane and held her tight.

Just then the bushes spread apart. Two little boys stepped out.

Indians!

Andi gasped. She let go of Taffy and jumped to her feet. Her heart gave a great big skip. She looked at Riley.

"I . . . I guess it's not so silly after all," he said in a scared voice.

That did not make Andi feel better. She wanted Riley to run after the Indians and chase them away. Far, *far* away.

But Riley didn't move. He didn't chase anybody. He stood in the creek, as frozen as a big block of ice.

The two little Indian boys didn't move either. They were staring at Andi and Riley. They each held a long spear. They had knives too.

One boy wore a grass skirt. The other boy wore a piece of cloth that hung down from his waist. They had strings of beads around their necks and bands on their heads. The bands held back their long, black hair.

For sure these are real, live Indians, Andi thought. *Just like in Riley's dime novel.*

Andi felt a chill go down her neck. She tried to swallow, but a lump got in the way. She tried to say something to Riley, but the lump would not let her words come out. She wanted to run away, but her feet would not obey.

She stood there, just as frozen as Riley.

For a long time, Andi and Riley stared at those Indian boys.

The Indian boys stared back.

Maybe we'll stare at each other until it gets dark, Andi thought. *Then Riley and I can sneak away.*

It was a good plan.

Then Andi remembered that she didn't know the way home—especially in the dark.

A loud yell made Andi jump.

A tall, older Indian boy crashed through the

bushes. He ran up to the two smaller boys. He talked to them in strange, fast words.

The boy in the grass skirt pointed at Andi and Riley.

The tall boy turned around. His eyes opened wide. He smiled. Then he said something that made the little boys laugh.

With a whoop, he rushed toward Andi and Riley.

Andi's feet suddenly obeyed. "Go away!" she screamed, splashing into the creek. This Indian would not capture *her!*

Then *whack!* She crashed into Riley. They both fell to the bottom of the creek.

But the tall Indian boy was not after Andi and Riley. Instead, he grabbed Midnight's mane and leaped onto the big horse's back.

Just like that.

Chapter 8

Too Many Indians!

"Get off my horse!" Riley yelled. He stood up and made his hands into tight fists.

Riley did not look scared now. He looked mad.

The Indian boy laughed. He rode Midnight up and down the creek bank, smiling the whole time.

Riley splashed out of the creek.

Andi stuck close to Riley. Her heart was pounding so hard it hurt. Her head hurt. Her stomach hurt.

Worst of all, she started crying.

It was no good. Andi could not make those drippy tears stop. The Indian boy was taking Midnight, and there was nothing she or Riley could do about it.

Andi cried louder. She didn't want the Indians to steal Midnight. She wanted to go home!

She blinked hard and looked at Riley. His face was red and all scrunched up. Only, he wasn't crying. He looked too mad to cry.

Just then Andi heard a loud voice—a grown-up's voice.

She gulped. Another Indian!

The Indian man was standing not too far away. He was dressed like the boys. He crossed his arms over his bare chest and spoke to the boy on Midnight.

Andi didn't know what the man was saying.

But the boy riding Midnight knew. He stopped smiling. He rode over to Riley and Andi. Then he slid off Midnight's back.

The man said a few more words.

The boy said something back. His shoulders slumped. He handed Midnight's reins to Riley.

"Please forgive my son," the man said. "He saw the black horse and wanted to ride him." He frowned at the boy. "But he should not have taken the horse without asking."

Andi kept crying. She couldn't stop. How many more Indians would sneak up on her?

The man walked over to Andi and knelt beside her. "Why are you crying?" he asked gently.

Andi backed away. Tears dripped down her face.

"She thinks you're going to make her an Indian captive," Riley said.

The Indian's mouth fell open. He looked very surprised. He put a hand on his chest and said, "The Yokuts are a peaceful people. We have never taken captives."

Just then the two little boys ran up. They peeked out from behind the man. Their eyes were big and dark.

"These are my sons," the man said. "They do not want to capture you, either. They want to play with you."

Andi was not so sure about that. She looked at the boy standing beside Midnight.

The Yokut man smiled. "Ku-yu only wants to ride the horse."

Riley reached into his back pocket and pulled out the dime novel. It was a wet, soggy mess. He handed it to the man.

"This is why Andi thinks she's going to be

captured," Riley said quietly. His face turned red. He looked like he wished he didn't have the dime novel.

The man looked at the cover for a long time. Then he let out a long, sad sigh. "I have heard of these books—these *dime novels*. There is no truth in their words. They are just made-up stories."

"That's what I keep telling her," Riley said. He shrugged, like he had never been scared at all.

Andi rubbed her tears away. She frowned at Riley. *You're acting too big for your britches again*, she wanted to say. *And in front of the Indians too!*

The man gave the book back to Riley. "My name is Lum-pa. We live farther up the creek. Come. I will show you."

Andi shook her head.

"We have to go home," Riley said. "Only . . . only . . ." He stopped talking and looked at the ground.

"Only, Riley doesn't know how to get home," Andi said. "That means we're lost. This probably isn't even the right creek."

Riley kept looking at the ground. "It's not," he whispered. "I just didn't want to tell you."

"It is easy to lose your way in these hills," Lum-pa said kindly. "And one creek looks very much like another."

Then he spoke to Ku-yu, who ran off as fast as a jackrabbit.

"He will tell the others that I bring guests," Lum-pa said. He held out his hand. "Come."

Andi did *not* want to go with Lum-pa. She wanted to go home. "Do you know where I live? It's the Circle C ranch. I'm Andi Carter, and I . . . I want to go home."

Lum-pa nodded. "I know the ranch. I know your family. But you have come far."

He pointed at the sun. It hung low in the sky. "It is too late to take you home today. We must wait for morning."

Andi felt shaky inside. She had to stay with the Indians—all night.

Just like an Indian captive.

Chapter 9

Yokut Camp

Andi had to think of something fast.

She ran to Taffy and threw her arms around her neck. "Taffy's little. She needs her mother's milk. I have to take her home."

Lum-pa smiled. "She might go hungry tonight, but that will not hurt such a big, strong foal."

"Andi's mother will be mighty upset if we don't show up back home," Riley said. "She'll skin me alive for getting Andi lost."

"Not when she learns you were with me," Lum-pa said.

Andi and Riley looked at each other. This Indian was not taking *no* for an answer.

Riley shrugged. "I guess we have to go with

him, Andi. We can't find the way home by ourselves."

So Andi and Riley picked up their socks and boots. Then Andi let Lum-pa put her on Coco. She let him put the two little Indian boys on Coco too. They squealed with joy.

Riley climbed up on Midnight.

Lum-pa led Coco and Midnight to the Yokut camp. Taffy followed close behind.

The camp was small and hidden away. There were two small huts and a campfire.

And there were baskets—lots of beautiful Yokut baskets. Some held acorns. Some held berries. One basket held beads and shells of different sizes.

Andi, Riley, and the two little boys slid off the horses.

Lum-pa took them over to the fire. Two Yokut women and three little girls were cooking something that smelled very good. Lum-pa talked to the women, but Andi didn't understand a word he was saying.

Besides, Andi's eyes were glued on what the women were doing. They were using sticks to drop rocks into a large basket of mush. They stirred and stirred. Then they dropped more rocks in the mush.

"Do these Indians eat rocks?" Andi whispered to Riley.

Riley was staring at the basket of rock mush too. "I don't know. But I sure hope they don't make *us* eat rocks."

Lum-pa chuckled and said something to the women. They laughed.

"Wa-see-it is my wife," Lum-pa explained. "She uses hot stones from the fire to heat the acorn mush." He grinned at Andi. "Who wants to eat cold mush?"

The two women were holding their sides and laughing. The little girls were giggling too.

Andi smiled. Then she giggled. Eating rocks *did* sound funny. She felt silly for thinking Indians ate rocks.

Looking at the family laughing together, Andi felt silly for thinking these Indians captured anybody.

She felt silly for being so scared.

"Come," Lum-pa said. "We will share our meal."

Eleven Yokuts sat around the fire. There was

even a baby. He kicked his fat brown legs and waved his arms.

Lum-pa looked up at the sky and said a few words.

Andi looked up at the sky too. "Are you praying to God?"

Lum-pa nodded. "Long ago, I learned about the Great Spirit and His Son, Je-sus, from a missionary. I also learned to speak English."

After that he handed Andi a small basket of the ground-up acorn mush. Then he gave her a piece of wood that looked like a spoon.

Andi stirred the mush and took a tiny taste. Then she took another taste. Pretty soon she was stuffing that good acorn mush into her mouth.

"This tastes better than oatmeal," she said with her mouth full.

"It sure does," Riley agreed.

Andi ate everything the Yokut people gave her: berries, deer stew, and another helping of acorn mush.

Riley ate even more than Andi.

When the meal was over, Riley ran to Midnight. He led his horse to Ku-yu and handed him the reins. "You can ride him any time you want."

Ku-yu smiled and clapped Riley on the shoulder. Then he mounted Midnight and galloped away.

The little boys and girls rode Coco. But mostly they fell off. Coco did not like five wiggly children on his back all at the same time. When he trotted, the children bounced and slipped off.

But they always climbed back on again.

Soon, the sun slipped behind the hills.

Andi snuggled next to Choo-nook, her new best friend. A coyote howled, but it was far away. The horses stirred. Taffy gave a little whinny.

Andi didn't hear any of it. She fell asleep.

And she didn't even dream about Indian captives.

Chapter 10

Good-bye

A fly buzzed next to Andi's ear.

She opened her eyes. The sun was shining through the hut's small door. It shone right in her face.

Andi sat up. Then she yawned and stretched.

Choo-nook was already awake. The little girl smiled at Andi. But she didn't say a word.

Andi didn't say a word either. She didn't know any Yokut words.

Only, it looked like Andi and Choo-nook didn't need any words. Choo-nook took off her shell necklace and hung it around Andi's neck. Then she pointed to Andi's head.

Andi rolled her eyes way up. Her red hair bow was hanging down over her forehead. She pulled it out and handed it to her new friend.

Choo-nook squealed and ran from the hut. She twirled the satin ribbon around and around, laughing the whole time.

After breakfast, the Yokut families gathered around Andi and Riley to say good-bye.

"I don't want to go home," Andi told Lum-pa.

"Neither do I," Riley said. "We're having too much fun."

Lum-pa laughed and told the others.

They shook their heads. "*Ohóm, ohóm.*"

"That means *no*," Lum-pa explained. "We do not want you to go, either. But your families are probably worried. They will be looking for you."

Lum-pa put Andi on Coco and helped Riley up on Midnight. Then he mounted up behind Riley.

They started on their way.

Coco whinnied. Taffy kicked up her feet and galloped to catch up with Coco. The little foal didn't look tired at all.

"No one would look for you at night," Lum-pa said. "But I am sure they started out as soon as the sun came up. We will meet them soon. But even if we do not, I will take you all the way to the ranch house."

"It's a long walk back to your camp without a horse," Riley said.

Lum-pa shrugged. "No matter."

They rode quietly for a long time in the bright morning sun.

Andi squirmed on Coco's back. There was something she had to tell Lum-pa—something important. She didn't want to, but she knew God wanted her to talk to her new friend.

Andi's words finally came out in a rush. "I'm sorry I thought you were going to capture me. I shouldn't have listened to that dime novel. Then I wouldn't have been so scared of you."

Lum-pa stopped Midnight.

Andi stopped Coco.

"I forgive you," Lum-pa said. "I think you have learned much."

Andi nodded. She waited for Lum-pa to nudge Midnight, but he didn't. He just sat there. His face looked sad.

"The truth is," Lum-pa said at last, "it is my people who are afraid of *your* people. Your people have killed many of my people. That is hard to forgive."

Andi looked at Riley. His eyes were big and full of surprise.

"Your father and I were friends," Lum-pa told Andi. "He helped me learn to forgive. He showed me how to give my anger to the Great Spirit and to His Son."

Andi waited quietly.

"Your father was a good man," Lum-pa said.

"We may live on his ranch for as long as we want. We hide so we can be safe and live in peace."

Just then Andi saw horses. There were four or five of them, and they were galloping fast. "Look!" she yelled.

Lum-pa's sad face turned smiley. He waved his arms and shouted. Then he slid off Midnight's back and ran to meet Andi's brothers.

"It has been a long time, my friends," Lum-pa said.

"*Too* long," Chad said, grinning.

They seemed happy to see each other.

Andi wasn't so happy.

Riley didn't look happy either. "I think we're in trouble," he whispered.

That's when Andi got a surprise. Her brothers were not mad. They were happy to see Andi. They were happy to see Riley too.

Justin pulled Andi off Coco. He hugged her tight. "We were on our way up to Lum-pa's camp to ask for help. But it looks like he already found you."

"I'm sorry I got us lost, Mr. Carter," Riley said in a small voice.

Chad was looking Taffy over. "Next time don't go so far." But he didn't sound mad—not even a little bit.

Justin reached out and grasped Lum-pa's arm. "Thank you, my friend."

Lum-pa nodded and turned to go.

"Wait," Chad said. "We brought along extra horses so your people could help us look for the kids. You should keep one."

"Sounds like a good trade to me," Justin said. He gave Andi another hug.

Lum-pa smiled at a glossy brown horse with its black mane and tail. "It is hard to say no to such a gift."

"Ku-yu's eyes will pop right out of his head when he sees it," Riley said.

Andi lifted her shell necklace. "Tell Choo-nook I'll come back to visit if Mother lets me."

Lum-pa smiled. "I will tell her."

"And," Andi said in a rush, "tell her that nobody's going to find you and hurt you if I can help it."

Justin gave Andi a puzzled look. "What are you talking about?"

Lum-pa laughed. Then he leaped on his new horse and galloped away.

"I'll tell you later, Justin," Andi said.

And she did.

A Peek into the Past

Does it seem strange that Andi and Riley went riding so far away—all by themselves? Well, in the 1800s, children had a lot more freedom than they have now. They also did a lot more work. Many children worked in factories. Others worked in the fields, picking crops. Some children took care of sheep and cows.

A six-year-old girl got lost in the same hills where Andi and Riley were lost. She was taking care of her family's sheep and went missing all night! Thankfully, she was found the next day.

The peaceful Yokut Indians lived in those same hills. It is true that some white men killed them. There was a bad law in California that made it easy to hurt the Indians. In 1874, when this story takes place, the Yokut Indians had to hide to keep their families safe.

And what about those dime novels? They were full of excitement, but the stories were wild and mostly made up. Many teachers and parents did not want children reading them. They felt the books put the wrong kind of ideas into young minds.

"Be careful, little eyes, what you see" is still true today.

Susan K. Marlow, like Andi, has an imagination that never stops! She enjoys teaching writing workshops, sharing what she's learned as a homeschooling mom, and relaxing on her 14-acre homestead in the great state of Washington.

Leslie Gammelgaard, blessed by the tall trees and flower gardens that surround her home in Washington state, finds inspiration for her artwork in the antics of her lively little granddaughter.

Grow Up with Andi!

**Don't miss any of Andi's adventures in the
Circle C Beginnings series**

Andi's Pony Trouble
Andi's Indian Summer
Andi's Fair Surprise
Andi's Scary School Days
Andi's Lonely Little Foal
Andi's Circle C Christmas

And you can visit www.AndiandTaffy.com
for free coloring pages, learning activities,
puzzles you can do online, and more!

For readers ages 9-14!

Andi's adventures continue in the Circle C Adventures series

Andrea Carter and the Long Ride Home
Andrea Carter and the Dangerous Decision
Andrea Carter and the Family Secret
Andrea Carter and the San Francisco Smugglers
Andrea Carter and the Trouble with Treasure
Andrea Carter and the Price of Truth

Check out Andi's Web site at
www.CircleCAdventures.com